# Doctor

Copyright © QEB Publishing, Inc. 2009

This edition published by Scholastic Inc., 557 Broadway,
New York, NY 10012, by arrangement with
QEB Publishing, Inc., 3 Wrigley, Suite A, Irvine, CA 92618

www.qeb-publishing.com

Library of Congress Cataloging-in-Publication Data

Askew, Amanda.
   Doctor / by Amanda Askew ; illustrated by
Andrew Crowson.
        p. cm. --  (QEB people who help us)
   ISBN: 978-1-59566-994-0 (hardcover)
  1.  Physicians--Juvenile literature.  I. Crowson,
Andrew, ill. II. Title.
   R690.A75 2010
   610--dc22
                                2009001989

ISBN: 978-1-59566-903-2 (paperback)

10 9 8 7 6 5 4 3 2 1

Printed and bound in China

**Author** Amanda Askew
**Designer and Illustrator** Andrew Crowson
**Consultants** Shirley Bickler and Tracey Dils

**Publisher** Steve Evans
**Creative Director** Zeta Davies
**Managing Editor** Amanda Askew

Words in bold are
explained in the
glossary on page 24.

# Doctor

Amanda Askew
Andrew Crowson

QEB

QEB Publishing

Meet Dr. Amar.
He is a doctor. He
helps to make sick
people feel better.

4

When Dr. Amar arrives at the office, Tanya is there. Tanya looks after the office and makes sure that everything is ready for when the **patients** arrive.

"Here's your mail."
"Thanks, Tanya."

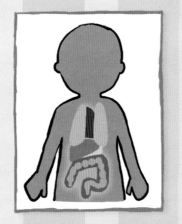

Dr. Amar goes into his office. He has a desk, chairs, bookshelves, and an examination table.

He looks at his computer to check which patients he will see today.

Dr. Amar's first patient is Rosie. She has a sore throat and a **fever**.

"Your throat is very red with yellow spots. You'll have to take a few days off from school and take some **medicine**."

Dr. Amar prints out a **prescription** from the computer and hands it to Rosie's dad.

"Please get this medicine from the **pharmacist**."

Next, Edward comes in. He has been getting headaches when he watches television or reads the newspaper.

Dr. Amar gives him an eye test.

"A, T... the others are a little blurry."

"I'd like you to visit an **optician** to see if you need glasses. Come back to see me if you're still getting headaches."

AT
FYH
UPOT
OAPD
ZXJMYU
AGQBHS

Dr. Amar sees about 15 people in the morning, but not everyone is ill.

Last week, Jane fell off her bicycle and cut her arm. She came back to see Dr. Amar today to check that her arm is **healing** properly.

"It's looking good. I'll put a clean **bandage** on and see you again next week."

Next, Rory and his younger brother come in for a check-up.

Rory is five years old.
"Hello, Rory. Step on
the scale for me.
You weigh 40 pounds
(18 kilograms). You're
growing quickly!"

Rory's brother is three years old. Dr. Amar gives him a special **shot** to keep him from getting serious illnesses.

"James, sit on Mommy's knee and read this book while I give you a shot."

"All finished! You were such a brave boy!"

17

In the afternoon, Dr. Amar
sees about 15 more people.

Salma has itchy **eczema** on her arms
that she cannot stop scratching.

Peter has a terrible earache.

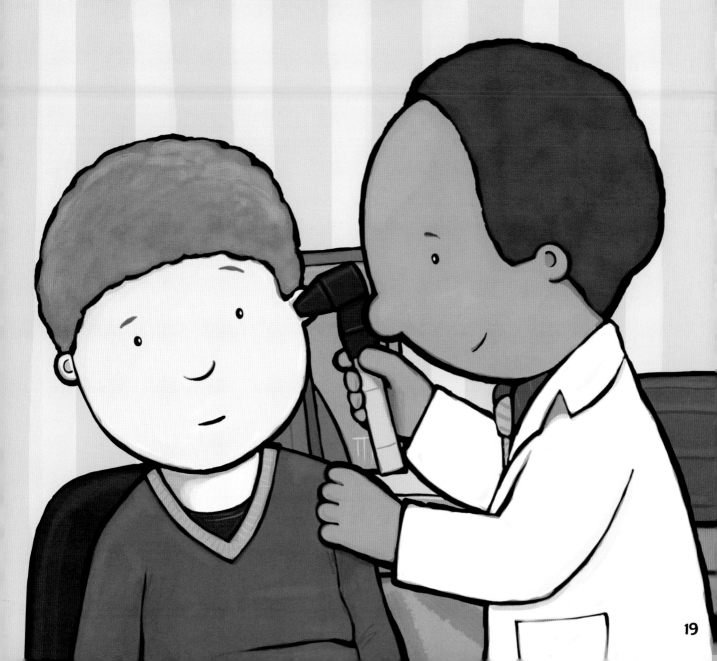

Brad has a rash.

Suzy has a
tickly cough.

21

Finally, Dr. Amar sees Tom. He has banged his thumb with a hammer. It's very red and swollen.

Dr. Amar cleans his thumb and wraps it in a bandage.

"Come back to see me if the swelling does not go down in a few days."

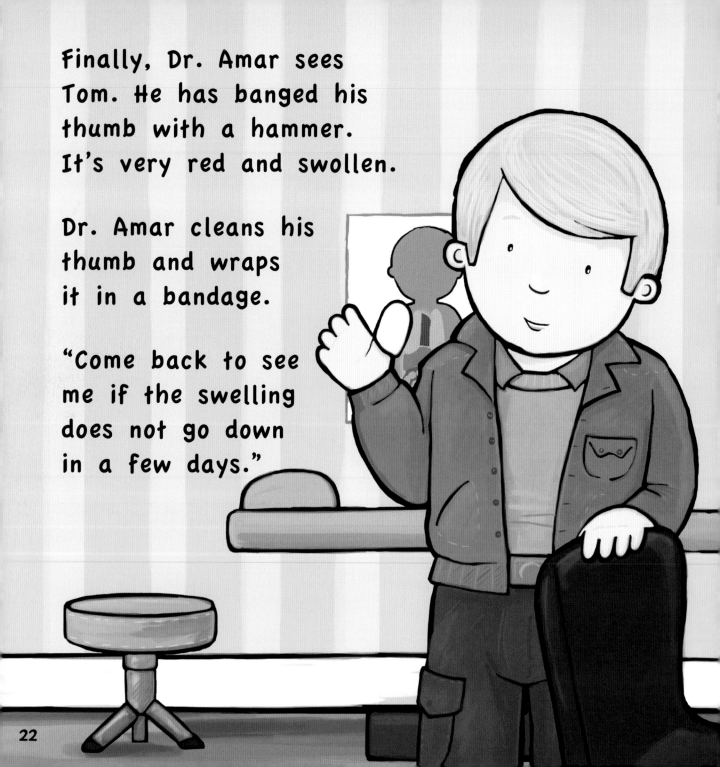

"Thanks, Doctor!"
"No problem.
Be more careful
next time!"

23

# Glossary

**Bandage** A piece of cloth that is tied around a cut to protect it.

**Eczema** Very red, swollen, and itchy skin.

**Fever** A high temperature.

**Heal** When skin or bone grows back and becomes healthy again.

**Medicine** A liquid or pill that someone takes to get well.

**Optician** Someone who checks that people can see properly.

**Patient** Someone who visits a doctor when he or she is sick.

**Pharmacist** A person who sells medicine.

**Prescription** A piece of paper that tells a pharmacist which medicine someone needs.

**Shot** When a needle is used to put medicine into someone's body.

## PEOPLE WHO HELP US

# Vet

Amanda Askew
Andrew Crowson

FLIP ME OVER

$5.99 US

ISBN: 978-1-59566-903-2

50599

9 781595 669032

Ages 3 and up
This edition is only available
for distribution through
the school market.

**SCHOLASTIC**

Printed in Guangdong, China
Scholastic Inc., New York, NY

www.scholastic.com

Library of Congress Cataloging-in-Publication Data

Askew, Amanda.
   Vet / by Amanda Askew ; illustrated by Andrew Crowson.
        p. cm. --  (QEB people who help us)
   ISBN: 978-1-59566-990-2 (hardcover)
   1.  Veterinarians--Juvenile literature.  I. Crowson, Andrew, ill. II. Title.
   SF756.A85 2010
   636.089'069--dc22

2009001993

Printed and bound in China

ISBN: 978-1-59566-903-2

10 9 8 7 6 5 4 3 2 1

**Author** Amanda Askew
**Designer and Illustrator** Andrew Crowson
**Veterinary consultant** Catheryn Hancock
**Consultants** Shirley Bickler and Tracey Dils

**Publisher** Steve Evans
**Creative Director** Zeta Davies
**Managing Editor** Amanda Askew

**Words in bold are explained in the glossary on page 24.**

People who help us

**Vet**

Amanda Askew
Andrew Crowson

QEB Publishing

Meet Dr. Beth.
She is a vet. She
helps sick and
hurt animals
get better.

Dr. Beth arrives at the **clinic** at about 8 o'clock in the morning. Clara looks after the office. She is chatting to Nurse Brown about today's **patients**.

5

First, Dr. Beth and Nurse Brown go to
the hospital to check on the animals.

"Barney's leg is healing well,"
Dr. Beth tells Nurse Brown.

"Harry's tummy is looking good after the lump was taken away."

Molly the cat had kittens last week. Some of the kittens could not suckle, so they came to the hospital to learn how to feed.

"How are you feeling, Molly? Your kittens are looking very well. I think you can go home today."

Then, Dr. Beth checks the
appointment book to see which
patients are visiting her today.

"It's going to be
a busy day, Clara!
Please send the
first patient in."

Charlie the cat
has been fighting
and has scratches
on his leg.

Daisy the dog needs
to have her claws
cut before they get
too long.

Thomas the turtle is not eating very well. This is because he has just finished **hibernating.**

12

Polly the puppy needs a **vaccination** to help her stay healthy.

Rosie the rabbit's teeth are too long. Dr. Beth will cut them for her.

Zuzu the snake just seems quiet.

Carly the cat has fleas. She has scratched her skin and it is sore.

Ronald the rat escaped from his cage and hurt his tail.

Dr. Beth's next patient
is a little more serious.
Dart the dog looks very
unhappy, and his owner
is worried.

"Dart won't eat, and
he has been sick."

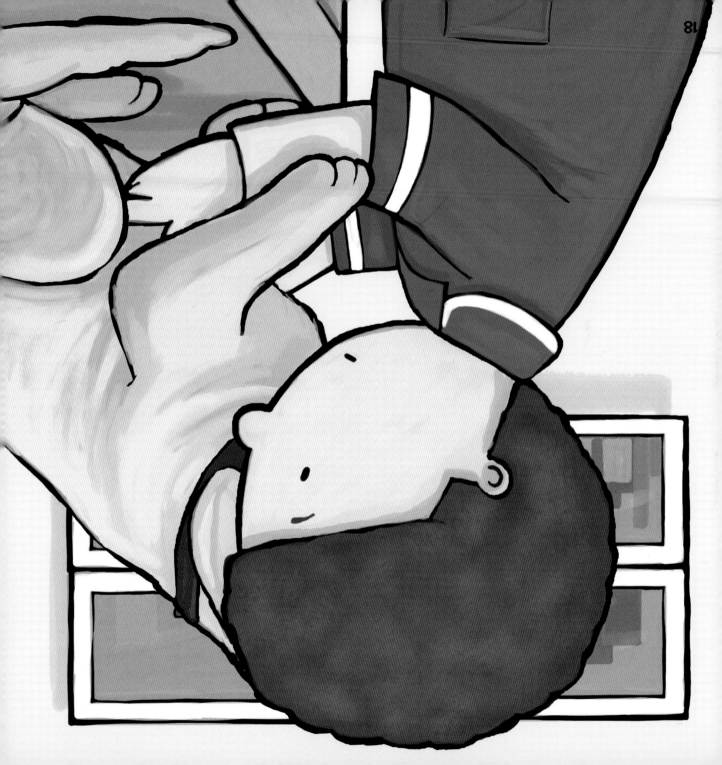

"He chews a lot
of things, but he's
never eaten any
of them before!"

"Let's see. Now,
I'm just going to
feel his tummy. Is
there a chance that
Dart could've eaten
something that he
shouldn't have?"

Dr. Beth sends Dart for an X-ray
with Nurse Brown, just in case.

Nurse Brown brings
the X-ray to Dr. Beth.

Nurse Brown takes
Dart to the hospital
and gets him ready
for the operation.

"It looks like Dart has
eaten a small ball.
He needs to have an
operation to remove it."

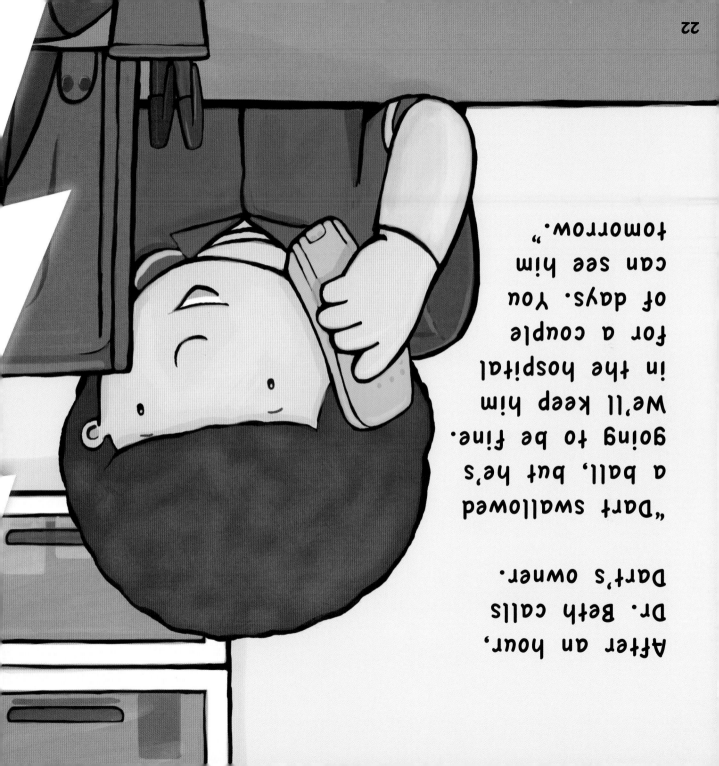

After an hour,
Dr. Beth calls
Dart's owner.

"Dart swallowed
a ball, but he's
going to be fine.
We'll keep him
in the hospital
for a couple
of days. You
can see him
tomorrow."

"Thank you so much," she says.

"No problem,"
Dr. Beth smiles.

# Glossary

**Clinic** A place where medical treatment is given.

**Heal** When skin or bone grows back and becomes healthy again.

**Hibernate** To go into a kind of deep sleep for winter.

**Operation** When someone's body is cut open to fix a part that is damaged.

**Patient** Someone who visits a doctor when he or she is sick.

**Suckle** To feed a young animal or baby with milk from its mother.

**Vaccination** When an animal or person is given a shot to protect him or her from a disease.

**X-ray** A photograph of the insides of something, such as bones inside the body.